MEET
MAGGIE
McMUDDLE

MEET MAGGIE McMUDDLE

MOIRA MILLER

Illustrated by Mairi Hedderwick

Methuen Children's Books

First published 1989
by Methuen Children's Books
Michelin House, 81 Fulham Road, London SW3 6RB
Text copyright © 1989 Moira Miller
Illustrations copyright © 1989 Mairi Hedderwick
Printed in Great Britain
by St Edmundsbury Press
Bury St Edmunds, Suffolk

British Library Cataloguing in Publication Data

Miller, Moira
Meet Maggie McMuddle
I. Title
823'.914 [J]

ISBN 0–416–13312–6

Contents

1
Meet
Maggie
McMuddle

It was one of those bright and bouncy days, and the birds were fairly shouting at the sunshine. The green front door of Number Forty, Antimacassar Street opened and out popped Maggie McMuddle, round and rosy, just like the lady from a weather house. But she had no time to stand around smiling at the sunshine.

She was all dressed up in her flowery overall, and carrying her big red plastic tidy-basket full of dusters and polish. It was spring cleaning day at Number Forty.

'Tut!' she said to Purpuss, who had followed her out. 'Just look at the finger-marks all over the letter-box. It's that mucky duck of a paper-boy. Must do something about that, right now!'

'Hmmm!' said Purpuss. He stretched out like a floppy ginger rug on the front windowsill. Someone had to do the important things, like keeping an eye on the street.

Without even stopping to look for her spectacles, Maggie McMuddle pulled a duster and a tin of polish from the basket and whizzed into action to clean up the brass letter-box.

She rubbed.

And huffed.

And buffed.

'My goodness, it IS warm,' she puffed.

Then she bundled up the duster, and she double-rubbed, until her fingers were nearly flat.

'Oh, dear. Oh, dearie me,' said Maggie McMuddle, as she stood back and looked at her work. 'I can't understand that.'

She took a deep breath and huffed on

8

the letter-box, and then she rubbed
again.

'I can't understand it at all,' said
Maggie McMuddle. 'It seems to have
gone all dark and dingy and it was so
lovely and shiny bright when I started.
Perhaps if I just put on a little more
polish...'

She dipped the duster in the tin
marked POLISH and rubbed, and scrubbed some more.

But the letter-box became duller and darker, and dirtier.

'Drat this clarty duster,' tutted Maggie McMuddle, and she popped indoors to find another one.

Along the sunny street came Big Tam the postman, skipping over the squares on the pavement, and whistling to the tune in his headphones. He stopped to sort through his bag.

'Bee-bop-ba-loo-back.
And one for Maggie Mac!'
'Hi-ya, Purpuss! How's business?'

He lifted the flap to push the letter through.

'Ooo-er,' said Big Tam, looking at his sticky black fingers.

'Oh, crikey!' he said, when he realised that he had put black marks all over the other letters he was holding. He tried to slide them back into his bag using two fingers of his clean hand.

But the bag was very heavy. It slipped off his shoulder, spilling letters all over the path. Big Tam twisted around, stepped back and trod on them, leaving dirty

footprints all over some of the envelopes.

'Help!' he gasped, and his grubby fingers smudged down the front of his bright yellow pullover, as he bent to pick up the letters.

The green front door opened again.

'Hello,' said Maggie McMuddle. 'Mercy me, you are in a state! Whatever have you been doing, laddie?'

"S not me, Mrs Mac, it's you,' wailed Big Tam, running his fingers through his hair and leaving dirty marks on his face. 'Look at the letter-box! And my new pullover. My Mum'll murder me, she's just finished knitting it!'

'Oh, dear me,' said Mrs McMuddle, peering at Tam's pullover. 'You are in a mess. Let me wipe you down, I've a clean duster here. I'll soon have that woolly tiddly bright.'

'No – no, that's all right, Mrs Mac,' said Big Tam, backing off down the steps and wiping his sticky fingers on the seat of his black trousers. He stuffed the last of the letters into his bag. 'I've got to get

12

on with my round. What have you been cleaning that letter-box with anyway? Shoe polish?'

'Shoe polish? You don't think I'd be that daft, do you?' Maggie McMuddle called after him. 'Well, do you?'

Big Tam smiled, shook his head and bounced off down the road whistling to himself again.

'Potty Postie!' said Maggie McMuddle, turning back to her polishing. She picked up two tins from the top of the red basket.

The tins came from the supermarket at the end of the road. They were both blue and white, and they both said POLISH in big bold letters. One was tightly shut – and the other was open.

'Ohhhhh!' said Maggie McMuddle slowly, and she reached into the pocket of her overall for her spectacles.

'Well – I wonder. . . ' said Maggie McMuddle, studying the tins closely.

'Surely I couldn't have been so silly,' said Maggie McMuddle, turning the tins around to read the other side.

The one with the lid screwed tightly shut said METAL. The open one said SHOE.

'Well fancy that,' giggled Maggie McMuddle. 'Big Tam was right, after all. I must have done the letter-box with my best Sunday shoe polish. What a messy muddle.'

She took her clean duster, and the tin marked METAL POLISH - she checked

it twice, with her spectacles on this time,
just to make sure. Then she rubbed.

And she scrubbed.

She huffed.

And she buffed.

        'Bee-bop-a-loo-bup.

        Got to get a shine up!'

sang Maggie McMuddle.

Then she bundled the duster into a ball
and rubbed and double-rubbed until her
fingers were nearly flat, and her brass
letter-box was the brightest in the whole
length of Antimacassar Street.

2
Maggie McMuddle and the Chocolate Cake

There were some days when Maggie McMuddle just could not make her mind up about anything. If she went up to the supermarket to buy a tin of soup, she would ask everyone she met what they liked best and end up either buying six tins or none at all.

One afternoon she found a recipe in a magazine for a particularly beautiful chocolate cake.

'Lovely and dark, with lots of thick butter icing in the middle, and some on top,' said Maggie McMuddle. 'Just the ticket for tea-time, Purpuss.'

'Hmmm,' said Purpuss. He was not all that fond of chocolate cake really, but he was always happy when the oven was on to do some baking, because then the old draughty kitchen was so much cosier.

Maggie McMuddle took out her big blue and white baking bowl, and went to the larder cupboard.

'Sugar, margarine, cocoa powder,' she counted out the packets. 'Two brown eggs, and flour.'

But there was no flour.

'Oh, foozle!' said Maggie McMuddle as

she searched through the cupboard. 'I remember now. I finished it when I made the scones. I'll just have to toot down to the supermarket for some more. There's plenty of time.'

She popped her nose out of the front door to see what the weather was doing. It was a winter day, but crisp and bright and sunny.

'Don't need a coat,' she said, and pulled on her big woolly cardigan. Then she picked up her shopping bag, took the key from the hook by the door, and off she went.

Mr Brown next door was slowly raking up leaves in his front garden.

'Trees,' he muttered. 'Nasty messy things, leaves falling all over the place.' He picked a fallen leaf off one of the ducks cut in his front hedge.

'Afternoon,' said Maggie McMuddle. 'Lovely day for the time of year, don't you think?'

Mr Brown stopped what he was doing, straightened up, and looked around him gloomily. 'Well,' he said slowly. 'It might be at the moment, but just you wait until the sun goes behind a cloud. Chilly wind that, chilly wind.'

'Oh dear, do you really think so?' Maggie McMuddle shivered, feeling colder already. 'Perhaps I'd better go back for my warm coat after all.'

'I should,' said Mr Brown, getting back to his raking. 'You can never be too careful.'

Maggie McMuddle went back up the

path, scrabbling about in the bottom of her bag for the key. She let herself in and pulled on her thick winter coat. Purpuss watched her lazily. The coat only just buttoned up on top of the cardigan.

'My, that's cosy. Feels better already,' she said, picking up her bag and setting off again.

"Bye Mr Brown.'

"Bye Mrs M.'

At the corner of the street, outside his dad's café, Sandy Sullivan was polishing his motorbike.

'Afternoon Sandy. Nice day – if a teensy bit chilly, don't you think?'

'Haaa,' said Sandy, breathing on the silver metal, and rubbing hard with his duster. 'Bound to rain.'

'Oh surely not,' said Mrs McMuddle.

'Always does when I polish the 'bike,' said Sandy giving a final rub to the mirror. 'Look at those clouds, they're all sitting up there waiting till I'm finished.'

'I see what you mean,' said Mrs McMuddle. There were just a few small grey clouds drifting across the sky.

'Perhaps I'd better just take a raincoat after all.'

She hurried off back home, rummaging through her bag and pockets for the front door key. At last she found it, and let herself in. Purpuss looked a little surprised as she pulled on her pink plastic raincoat over the winter coat and tried to fasten the poppers. Each time she bent to do the bottom one, the top ones pinged open again.

'Oof, this coat is getting a little bit tight,' she gasped. 'Perhaps I need a new one.'

She picked up her bag, shut the door and set off again.

"Bye Mr Brown.'

"Bye Mrs M.'

'Goodbye Sandy.'

'Toodle-oo, Auntie Mac.'

Round the corner she went, and along to the crossing at the park gates. A painter was busy at work on the railings.

'Nice afternoon,' said Mrs McMuddle. 'A wee bit cold, and it might rain, but it's really rather pleasant.'

'A WEE bit cold!' said the painter. 'I've been working on these railings all afternoon. Haven't had a tea-break yet, Missus, and I'm frozen! It's cold enough for snow if you ask me.'

'Snow!' Mrs McMuddle was in a real tizzy. 'Oh dear, that would fairly ruin my good shoes. I think I'd better just slip home and change into my wellington boots.'

So back she hurried. Past the painter, past Sandy Sullivan, polishing his bike, and Mr Brown slowly raking the leaves in his garden. Back up her own front path, rummaging in her bag, and through all her pockets.

'Drat that key, where does it get to?' At last she found it, let herself in and sat down, puffing and gasping to pull on her wellington boots. Purpuss stood up and walked round in a circle on his toes, with his legs stiff, just to show that he was a little annoyed at being woken up again.

'I can hardly see my feet,' puffed Maggie McMuddle. 'Never mind pull my boots on. Just as well I don't have to tie laces.' At the front door she turned back and added a warm hat and a scarf.

'Just to be sure,' she said, looking at herself in the hall mirror. 'Now the weather can do what it likes, I'm ready for anything.' She squeezed through the front door and off down the path.

''Bye Mr Brown.'

''Bye Mrs M.'

'Goodbye Sandy.'

'Toodle-oo.'

'Goodbye painter. I hope you feel warmer soon.'

'Tara, luv. Should do, I'm clocking off in ten minutes.'

Opposite the park gate, P.C. Peters was on traffic duty. She smiled and nodded. Mrs McMuddle waited until all the cars stopped, and then she stepped off the pavement to cross to the supermarket.

'Lovely day, isn't it?' said P.C. Peters. 'Just like spring again.' Mrs McMuddle stopped, right there in the middle of the road and stared up at her.

'Oh! Do you really think so?' she said.

23

'You don't think it's a wee bit cold?'

'I'm warm enough!'

'Or that it might rain?'

'Rain? No chance!'

'Or snow even?'

'Never!' laughed P.C. Peters. 'It's a lovely day.'

'Um – oh dear,' Mrs McMuddle looked

at the supermarket across the road, then she turned back.

'Back in a tick,' she called, leaving P.C. Peters to sort out all the traffic.

She hurried back up Antimacassar Street, past the painter, past Sandy Sullivan, still polishing his motorbike, past Mr Brown raking up the last of the leaves.

She puffed up the front path, frantically searching for her key.

'I know I had it when I came out. It was in my bag. No, maybe I put it in my raincoat pocket, or in my heavy coat pocket, or my cardigan. . . ' She found it at last, and let herself in.

Purpuss completely ignored her.

'Oof,' she gasped, pulling off her boots, raincoat, scarf, hat and the heavy winter coat. 'That feels much better. I knew it was going to be a nice day. Now I'd better hurry if I'm going to get to the shops on time.'

And off she set once more. No Mr Brown, he had finished dusting his front path and gone indoors. No Sandy, he was sitting in the café, with a mug of tea, admiring his shiny bike. Round the corner, past the park, there was a WET PAINT sign on the railing, but the painter had gone. Along to the crossing, and P.C. Peters had gone off duty. Mrs McMuddle waited until the road was clear and then trotted across to the supermarket, just in time to see the manager putting up the 'CLOSED' sign.

'Oh bother!' she said. 'I've left it too late. That's what comes of letting other people make up your mind for you, and I was so looking forward to that chocolate cake, too.'

'I am sorry, madam,' said the manager. 'Was it something special you wanted?'

'Flour,' said Maggie McMuddle, following him back into the shop before he had a chance to close the door. 'I was going to do some baking, but I found that I'd run out of flour. . . '

The manager put his glasses on the end of his nose and began to hunt along the shelves.

'. . . and then I met Mr Brown, and he said it was going to be cold, so I had to go back for my warm coat. . . '

'Self-raising or plain?' said the manager.

'Plain . . . but then when I met Sandy Sullivan, he thought it might rain – well it did look a bit like it at the time . . . '

'White or wholemeal?'

'White, please . . . and then the painter

27

at the park said it felt like snow. Well, really I said, but I had to go back and change into my boots, just in case. Better safe than sorry. . . '

'Large or small?'

'Large . . . and P.C. Peters said it was just like spring, and there was me, all wrapped up like a Christmas parcel. That's lovely, dear, just pop it in my bag and I'll toddle off home now.'

'Good thing you caught me in time,' said the manager as Maggie McMuddle counted out the right money.

'That's true. I might not have been able to bake my cake, and it's all my own silly fault for allowing other people to change my mind once I've made it up. I won't do it again. Not ever.'

'Very wise, madam,' said the manager, letting her out. 'What sort of cake is it?'

'Chocolate of course, with lots of thick butter icing. That's my favourite.'

'Really?' said the manager, locking the door behind them. 'I prefer cherry cake myself. All that lovely juicy fruit. Mmmm!'

28

Maggie McMuddle waved as he walked off down the road, then she looked both ways, very carefully, and crossed to the park gates.

'Cherry cake? Well,' she thought as she walked past the railings and turned the corner into Antimacassar Street.

'Haven't had one of those for a long time. Make a nice change from chocolate,' she thought as she passed the corner café.

'I don't know. . . ' she said to herself. She waved to Mr Brown who was standing in his front window staring gloomily out into the garden at the leaves blowing down from the trees across the road.

'Maybe I will . . . ' She rummaged in the bottom of her bag for the front door key.

'But I wonder if I've got enough cherries. . . ?'

3
Maggie McMuddle's Washing Day

One Monday morning Maggie McMuddle woke up early, opened the curtains and sniffed. It had rained during the night, but now the sky was fresh and scrubbed clean, and the little clouds were playing Catch As Can.

'It's just the day for washing blankets,' she said, and she dressed quickly. It would have been even more quickly but she couldn't find her slippers.

'Drat the things, why are they always disappearing, just when I need them?' She poked under the bed and Purpuss shot out, squalling. He had been sleeping

on top of the slippers and didn't take too kindly to being woken up.

'Hoots toots, pussy!' said Maggie McMuddle. 'Someone got out from under the wrong side of bed today.' She wiggled her toes into the nice warm slippers and went downstairs.

After breakfast she plugged in her old washing machine, stuck the hose on the tap and turned on the hot water. While the tub was filling she stripped all the blankets from the beds.

There was a pink blanket from her

own bed, a navy blue one from the bunk-bed in the tiny box room, and a yellow blanket that matched the roses on the wallpaper in the big spare bedroom. She took them all down to the kitchen and as she waited for the machine to fill she poured another cup of tea and looked around.

'Oh dear,' she sighed. 'I really meant to scrub that floor first. It could do with it, but my old knees are so stiff just now.'

'Mrrr,' grumbled Purpuss. He was still annoyed at having been woken up in the middle of a good dream.

'It's a pity the washing machine couldn't do that for me while it's at the blankets,' said Maggie McMuddle as she stuffed them into the tub and switched on the machine. She was just tipping in some soap powder when there was a rat-a-tat-tat at the front door.

'G'Morning!' shouted Big Tam the postman. He always shouted when he wore his headphones. 'Lovely day for it! Couple of letters and a card asking if you want your windows replaced.'

'Not today, thanks,' shouted Maggie McMuddle. 'I'm putting my blankets out on the line.'

'Time?' shouted Big Tam. 'It's ten past nine.' And off he bopped to deliver next door's football coupon.

'Dozy dumpling,' sniffed Mrs McMuddle. 'Now let's see what we've got here.' She was rummaging through the old biscuit tin where she kept all her bits and bobs and spare spectacles when she suddenly remembered the blankets.

'Did I put soap powder in there?' she asked Purpuss. 'Really, I'm getting so forgetful.'

But Purpuss, who usually kept an eye on these things, was still sulking. He kept his beady green eyes tight shut and pretended to be fast asleep.

'Probably not,' said Mrs McMuddle, tipping in some more powder, and off she puffed upstairs to make up the beds again.

'Coo-ee!' called a voice from the kitchen five minutes later.

'That sounds like Doris-next-door,'

33

sighed Maggie McMuddle. 'Better see what she wants.' Mrs Brown was standing in the kitchen, beside the washing machine.

'Can't stay, Maggie dear. Just brought round some of Angus's home-grown, prize-winning tomatoes,' said Mrs Brown proudly, putting the bowl on the kitchen table.

'That's very kind of you,' said Mrs McMuddle.

'Oh, my pleasure I'm sure. Only too pleased to help a neighbour,' said Mrs Brown. 'Speaking of which . . . '

But before she could finish, the doorbell rang and Mrs McMuddle didn't hear her add, 'I just popped a little more soap powder in the machine for you,' before she went back next door again.

Charlie the gas man was standing on the front door step.

'Come to read the heater meter, ducks,' he said.

'In the kitchen, Charlie,' sighed Mrs McMuddle. 'Just carry on while I finish off these beds.'

Charlie had to move the washing machine a little to get into the corner cupboard.

'Oh, crumbs!' he said, as he knocked over the soap packet, and powder spilled all over the floor.

Quickly, before Mrs McMuddle came back downstairs, he scooped up the spilt powder and tipped it into the washing machine.

Slish-slosh, gurgle-gurgle, gloop, went the machine, sounding rather as if it had overeaten.

Purpuss, in his basket beneath the table, stretched, raised an eyebrow, decided there was nothing to worry about, and went back to sleep again. By the time Mrs McMuddle came downstairs, Charlie was reading the meter as though nothing had happened.

'That's me done,' he said. 'Tara.' And he went off down the road.

'What a morning,' puffed Maggie McMuddle. 'It's busier than a bus station in this house.' And she sat down for a few minutes in her comfy armchair.

Slish-slosh, slish-slosh went the washing machine. Maggie McMuddle began to feel quite sleepy. Slish-slosh, slish-slosh, slishhhhhh. Her eyes slowly closed and she slipped off to sleep.

Slishhhh-sloshhhh, slishhhh-sloshhhh-slishhhh.

Shloooooomp.

Whirrrrrrrrrrrrrr.

Gloopita-gloopita-gloopita, gurgle-gurgle, gurgle.

Guloooop! The washing machine hiccupped very loudly.

Purpuss shot out of his basket with a very loud 'Meeeeeeerrraow!' and jumped on top of the fridge.

'Gracious goodness, what was that?' gasped Maggie McMuddle waking up suddenly.

She opened the kitchen door, and stopped, and gawped.

There were bubbles everywhere. Bubbles round the cooker, bubbles round the fridge. The kitchen table was an island in a sea of bubbles. There were still more bubbles blowing in a stream out of the

36

RULES
OF THE
KITCHEN

September

back door into the garden. And in the middle of the bubble muddle sat the washing machine, glooping and gurgling and pouring out even more bubbles. The whole kitchen seemed to be knee-deep in fluff.

'Help! Help!' screeched Maggie McMuddle, so loudly that Mrs Brown, Big Tam and Charlie the gas man, all came running up the path and into the kitchen to see what had happened.

What a kerfuffle! There was Maggie McMuddle slipping and sliding. The washing machine was guloopiting about on the wet floor, spilling out more and more froth. Purpuss was perched on top of the fridge, squalling furiously. His saucer of milk and basket were some-where underneath all the bubbles.

'Having a spot of bother then, Mrs Mac?' said Big Tam. He pulled off his shoes and socks, rolled up his trousers, and waded through the foam to switch off the washing machine. He started to laugh, as he waded back out through the foam, and the others joined in.

'It's not funny,' gasped Maggie McMuddle, but she was laughing just as much as the others. 'Just look at my kitchen. However could that have happened?'

And then she remembered that she must have put two lots of soap powder into the machine when Big Tam came to the door.

'Oh!' said Mrs Brown, 'I put some in, too. Just trying to be helpful like.'

'Hem!' Charlie the gas man coughed and went quite pink. Then he explained about knocking over the packet and sweeping up the spilt powder.

'It seems to be all our fault,' said Big Tam. 'So I think we'd better help you mop up.'

They rolled up their sleeves to help Maggie McMuddle clean up the kitchen. Big Tam and Charlie the gas man rinsed out the blankets and hung them on the line. Mrs Brown helped to make tomato sandwiches and coffee all round for lunch.

After they had all gone Maggie

McMuddle went into the kitchen to wash up the cups and plates.

'Ah well,' she said, looking around at her shining bright and incredibly clean kitchen floor. 'I suppose the washing machine did get the kitchen floor scrubbed for me after all. In a sort of way.'

'Meeeeeawoooo,' said Purpuss thankfully, and he rubbed against her leg as she poured fresh milk into his newly washed dish. He was so pleased to see the kitchen back to normal he quite forgot his sulks.

4
Maggie McMuddle and the Chinese Feast

One morning Mrs McMuddle came downstairs to find a card and a letter lying on the mat.

The card was from a cleaning firm.

LET US MAKE YOUR OLD
FURNITURE LOOK LIKE NEW.
UPHOLSTERY CLEANED –
WOODWORK STRIPPED
AND POLISHED.

'We could do with that, Purpuss,' said Maggie McMuddle. 'The parlour is beginning to look very grubby.'

Purpuss growled. He knew that if the chairs and sofa were cleaned he wouldn't

be allowed to lie on them. Not for ages anyway.

'No? Well, maybe not. Let's see what the letter is then.

It was an interesting-looking envelope, blue with a red-striped border and AIR MAIL printed in the corner.

'Oooh, how exciting,' she said. She knew immediately, by the writing, that it was from her nephew Albert.

Albert was a sailor, and had been right

round the world and back again with his
ship. He had visited places Mrs McMuddle had hardly even heard of and she
loved it when he came home to spend a
week or two in the tiny attic box bedroom.

'You're the height of nonsense, Albert,'
she had said to him. 'Far too big for this
little room.'

'Nonsense, Auntie Maggie!' Albert's
laugh rattled the roof tiles just above
their heads. 'Cabin like this is just
ticketty-boo for a sailor on leave.' He
hugged her so hard her feet came right
off the floor. Then he would sit down to
eat a huge tea, and tell her about all the
wonderful places his ship visited.

'Hong Kong,' said Albert dreamily.
'That's a place to sling your hammock!
It's right round the other side of the
world, and full of such sights and sounds
and smells.' He finished the last of the
egg sandwiches and helped himself to a
scone.

'D'you know, we all went out to dinner
one night, but not like here. We sat on

cushions on the floor round a big low table, and what food we had! It all looked like it was something else. There was red and yellow rice like confetti. And crispy rolled-up pancakes, like little brown parcels of vegetables all ready for posting. And soup made from flower petals. I'm telling you, Auntie Maggie, it was a real banquet, a feast fit for an Oriental potentate.'

'Fancy that!' Maggie McMuddle was wide-eyed with amazement as she refilled the big brown teapot. 'I'd love to do that, but I don't suppose I ever will.'

Albert laughed.

'Hong Kong's all right, Auntie Maggie, but there's nothing like coming home to one of your totally scrumptious high teas.'

He dolloped strawberry jam and cream on his scone, and told her about the time he visited the penguins at the South Pole, and had kippers for breakfast in an igloo.

Maggie McMuddle loved his stories.

'He's every bit as good as the telly,' she

44

always said to the Browns.

So of course, when Albert's air mail letter came, she popped her glasses on and sat down to enjoy it with her tea and toast.

'Dear Auntie Maggie,' said the letter,

'I know this is a bit short notice, but my ship comes home at the end of next week – Saturday that is.

'I do hope it is not an inconvenience, but I should love to drop in and please may I bring some of my shipmates with me this time? I have told them all about your scones and jam, and they would very much like to come to tea.

'Best love and a big hug, Your ever loving nephew, Albert.'

'Well. My goodness!' gasped Maggie McMuddle. 'That Albert! Whatever will he do next? Coming here with a whole ship-load of sailors. I don't know. What do you think, Purpuss?'

Purpuss stretched and yawned and flicked the tip of his tail.

'Very sensible,' she said. 'Nothing to get in a flap about. Well he did say the end of NEXT week, so that gives me plenty of time to get ready.' She ticked off the days on the calendar.

'This is Friday, so they'll be here one week tomorrow. All these visitors, and the parlour's looking so dingy. It really needs a proper spring clean, and I don't have time. I know, where's that card that came this morning? I'll get them to come and take away the chairs and settee for cleaning. That'll soon freshen things up.'

Purpuss sighed, and crept off to sleep under the sideboard. He hated it when people moved things around.

The next morning, Saturday, Maggie McMuddle was up early. She buttoned on her busy overall, and bustled about polishing and dusting until even Purpuss was frightened to come into the house, in case he was polished by mistake. She took down all the pictures and the curtains, and the men from the cleaning firm came and took away the chairs and settee.

She was standing on the kitchen stool, dusting the picture rail when she heard voices at the front door.

Lots of voices!

There seemed to be laughter and the sound of several pairs of heavy boots, crunch crunch crunch, on the front path. And then the door-knocker rattled. Rat-a-tat-tat!

'Hello, Auntie Maggie. You there?' Albert shouted. 'The fleet's in port!'

Maggie McMuddle nearly fell off the stool. She tripped over her feather duster and trod on Purpuss in her hurry to answer the door. She opened it wide, and there stood — Albert.

Not only Albert, but Albert and six suntanned sailors all talking and laughing, and looking very hungry.

'Hello, Auntie Maggie,' he shouted, giving her a hug that lifted her right out of her slippers. 'This is Joe and Sam and Duffy and Nobby and Ginger and Fruit-cake.'

'Delighted to come aboard,' said Joe, snapping a smart salute.

'Pleased to transfer the cargo, ma'am,' said Sam, shyly handing her a large bunch of white daisies wrapped in blue paper.

'Splice the mainbrace!' laughed Duffy and Nobby handing over an interesting-looking bottle.

'And so say Ginger and Fruitcake,' said the last two sailors, holding out a huge box of chocolates.

'Fruitcake?' said Maggie McMuddle faintly, 'and Ginger? Oooh, bless me, Albert, I'm all of a tiswas. You're not supposed to be here. Not until next Saturday. That's what your letter said.'

'No it wasn't,' said Albert indignantly, putting her down again.

'Yes it was, my lad!' Maggie McMuddle pulled the letter from her overall pocket and pointed to the words. '"My ship comes home at the end of next week – Saturday that is." That's what you said.'

'But, Auntie Maggie, I wrote that letter LAST week, so this IS next week – if you see what I mean.' All the sailors tried to explain at once, until Maggie McMuddle's head was spinning like a top.

48

'Oh, Albert,' she wailed. 'Whatever are we going to do? What a kerfuffle. I've sent off all the furniture for cleaning, and there's no food in the house. At least not enough to feed all your friends.'

'Never fear, Auntie Maggie,' said Albert, and he turned and whispered something to the six big smiling sailors behind him on the path.

'Will do!' they shouted.

'Wilco!'

'Aye, aye, sir!'

'Yo-ho!'

'Anchors aweigh!'

They all nodded, swung round on their heels and swept off down the road like a ship in full sail.

'Don't worry,' called Albert hurrying after them. 'Everything will turn out all right. You'll see. The Navy's here!'

Maggie McMuddle stood speechless, shaking her head.

'Put the kettle on!' shouted Albert. 'We'll be back before you can get the steam up.'

And so they were.

Ten minutes later Albert and Joe and Sam and Duffy and Nobby and Ginger and Fruitcake clumped into the parlour, carrying paper bags full of strange greaseproof paper packets and silver tinfoil dishes.

'We've been to Charlie Ching's up the

High Street and brought you back a Chinese feast,' said Albert. 'Let's scoff it while it's nice and hot.'

So Maggie McMuddle, and Albert and Joe and Sam and Duffy and Nobby and Ginger and Fruitcake all sat in a ring on cushions on the parlour floor.

Albert handed round plates and forks. He put the little silver dishes on a cloth in the middle of the ring, and then he took the tops off.

'Mmmmmmmmmm!' said Maggie McMuddle and all the sailors together.

What a wonderful smell. And what a delicious sight it was. There was rice, coloured red and yellow like confetti, and tiny parcels of crispy stuffed pancakes, and chicken and prawns and strange crispy crackers and bamboo shoots.

'It's a feast fit for an Oriental potentate!' said Maggie McMuddle, and she and the sailors didn't need to be invited twice to help themselves.

'There you are, Auntie Maggie,' said Albert, when they had all finished and Purpuss was licking up the last scraps. 'Now you know just what it's like to go out to dinner in Hong Kong, and you didn't even have to go over your own front doorstep to do it!'

'Quite, quite delicious,' said Maggie McMuddle. 'But you must all come back for a proper tea tomorrow night.'

'With scones,' said Albert.

'And home-made strawberry jam,' said Joe.

'With cream, lots of it!' sighed little fat Sam.

'And egg sandwiches,' said Nobby.

'With salad cream,' added Duffy.

'And fruitcake and ginger?' said the last two sailors.

'And fruitcake and ginger,' promised Maggie McMuddle.

5
Maggie McMuddle's Bicycle

One Friday afternoon, Maggie McMuddle came struggling back down the road with the weekend shopping.

'Oof!' she said, parking her bags on the front door step while she hunted for her key. 'I'm fair puggled. It's a long walk back with all this stuff.'

'You want to get yourself a bicycle,' said Mr Brown. He was out in his front garden, trimming the hedge into the shape of a row of fat green ducks. 'My Doris used to have a lovely one, with a big basket on the front.'

'I never thought of that, I must say,'

said Maggie McMuddle doubtfully. 'There is an old bike out in the shed, but it hasn't been out since – ooh – not since Purpuss was a kitten. It's probably got two flat tyres now, and besides, I don't think . . .'

But Mr Brown liked nothing better than tinkering with old machinery.

'You pop the kettle on for a cuppa,' he said, dropping his clippers. 'I'll soon fix it up right as ninepence for you.'

They had to empty the shed completely

to find the bicycle. Purpuss, who had been snoozing happily among the junk, miaowed crossly, stalked out and lay on top of the garden wall watching them. All the garden tools were pulled out, a one-legged wheelbarrow – 'Must fix that for you sometime,' said Mr Brown – the old lawnmower, and all the bits and bobs that might come in useful some day.

'I really must throw some of this away,' said Maggie McMuddle, quickly trying to push an upturned cardboard box over a rusty pair of handlebars that poked out from the heap.

But there was no stopping Mr Brown.

'Why there's your bike, Mrs Mac. Fancy! You almost covered it up just now.'

'Just fancy!' sighed Maggie McMuddle. The bicycle looked rather ramshackle and rusty. 'I don't think this is a very good idea. Perhaps we should just put it back and forget all about it.'

'Nonsense!' said Mr Brown, and he went to fetch his tool-box and some little rubber patches to mend the two flat tyres.

He worked on it for the whole morning. Purpuss lay on top of the shed roof and watched with interest.

'Please don't worry too much about it,' said Maggie McMuddle when she took out some tea and sandwiches at lunch-time. She tiptoed through the pile of oily nuts and bolts on the path. 'I don't mind walking to the shops, Mr Brown. Really.'

'Nothing beats Angus Brown,' he muttered, leaving oily fingermarks all over the sandwiches.

And it didn't. By tea-time the brakes and tyres were repaired.

'It does look a bit tatty though,' he admitted. 'Have to do something about that.'

'There's no hurry,' said Maggie McMuddle, but he had already gone.

On Saturday morning, bright and early, Sandy Sullivan from the corner café was on the doorstep with his radio under his arm and a paint pot in one hand. His fuzzy spike of blue hair stood straight up, just like the brush in his other hand.

'Mr Brown told me about your bike,

Auntie Mac, and I've brought some paint along. Smashing colour, electric blue, same as me motorbike.'

'Em – yes, awfully nice of you, Sandy,' said Maggie McMuddle doubtfully. 'It's a little bit – BRIGHT, isn't it?'

'They'll see you coming then. Be able to jump out of your way quicker like.'

'I don't know. I don't think this is a very good idea,' said Maggie McMuddle.

'Go on,' said Sandy. 'It's great!' He disappeared down the path to the garden shed, switched on the radio, very loudly, and howled along with the music as he worked. Just before tea-time he popped his head around the kitchen door.

'That's me done,' he called. 'Looks a real treat, but don't touch it, the paint's still wet.'

'Don't worry,' muttered Maggie McMuddle, but he didn't hear her.

'Oh, I nearly forgot,' he stopped at the gate. 'Old Dozy Duncan up the road will be along in the morning with some lights. He doesn't need them since he and the missus bought the new tandem.

58

They're a bit old-fashioned, but they're just the ticket for you.'

'Oh – thanks very much, I'm sure,' said Mrs McMuddle, but Sandy had gone.

Sure enough, on Sunday morning bright and early, there were Dozy and Mrs Duncan, all kitted up in matching baggy shorts, long rainbow-striped pullovers and little knitted toorie-hats to match. He was carrying a huge plastic bag.

'That's never a set of lights for the bike!' gasped Maggie McMuddle. 'It'll look more like a football stadium with what you've got in there.'

'No, it's not just the lights.' Dozy laughed. 'It's a basket from Mrs Fairbairn, off her old bike. She kept it for Fandango to sleep in, but he didn't like it and she had to buy a new one with a proper quilt and everything. It's only a little bit chewed.'

He fitted the old lights and basket on the bike and then stood back to admire his handiwork.

'Lovely,' he said. 'Me and Mother are

off out for the day now on the tandem.
You could join us next week.'

'No, I don't really think . . .' said
Maggie McMuddle, but Dozy and Mrs
Duncan had gone.

'Oh dear,' said Maggie McMuddle,
shaking her head. 'They'll all be so
disappointed if I don't use that bicycle.
And I don't think I want to.'

'In fact,' she said to Purpuss at tea-
time, 'I KNOW I don't want to. But how
do I tell them it's not a good idea, when
they've all gone to so much trouble?'

'Hmmm,' said Purpuss. He needed
time to think about the problem.

Next morning was Monday, and Mrs
McMuddle had to go shopping.

'Not taking the bike then?' called Mr
Brown.

'Oh!' she jumped. 'I didn't see you down
there behind the hedge.'

'Just having a stern word with the
weeds,' said Mr Brown, and he stood and
watched as Maggie McMuddle pushed
the bicycle out to the road.

'My word!' he said. 'It does look quite

MAGNIFICENT. There's no getting away from that.' Maggie McMuddle had to agree.

The silver wheels were gleaming and polished, Sandy's electric blue paint seemed even brighter out in the sunshine, the big old-fashioned lamps glittered, and even the rather battered basket looked smarter.

'Well go on then,' urged Mr Brown, as Mrs Brown came out to watch.

'Come on, Auntie Mac,' shouted Sandy. He came running up to help Mr Brown hold the bicycle steady as Maggie McMuddle climbed on.

Dozy Duncan and his missus came out, parked their tandem by the pavement and came over to offer advice.

'One, two, three, GO!' said Mr Brown and they all pushed. Maggie McMuddle pedalled furiously and wobbled off down the road.

'I still don't think this is a very good idea . . .' she called. But nobody heard her, except Purpuss who suddenly spotted his pet hate, Mrs Fairbairn's fat poodle, Fandango. He shot off the wall, and dived across the road right in front of the bicycle.

'MIND MY DUCKS!' yelled Mr Brown as Maggie McMuddle swerved, rattled up on to the pavement and headed straight for his hedge. She bounced off, squashing the middle duck.

'Ooooh, help,' she wailed, and wobbled unsteadily back across the road again. Aiming straight at the beautiful, gleaming tandem parked outside the Duncan's house.

Dozy and his missus leapt into action as the tandem fell over with a clatter.

'Somebody stop me!' shouted Maggie McMuddle as she wobbled on down the street.

'Mind my bike!' yelled Sandy, tearing after her. He caught up in time to catch her as she wobbled to a crashing stop against his motorbike.

'Oh, Auntie Mac,' moaned Sandy. 'Look what you've done to my lovely paintwork.'

*

Later, much later, after they had all had a settling-down cup of tea and a ginger biscuit around Maggie McMuddle's kitchen table, they left to tidy up the damage. Mr Brown, who was last to go, stopped on the doorstep and shook his head.

'Perhaps that wasn't such a good idea of yours after all, Mrs McMuddle. I'll just pop the bicycle back in the shed for you.'

And he went off to do that, leaving Maggie McMuddle and Purpuss, for once, both absolutely speechless.

6
Maggie McMuddle's Mystery Tour

Cousin Annie Flora was coming to stay for two weeks. She had sent a post card from Drumtoochtie to tell Maggie McMuddle when she would be arriving off the bus. On the other side was a picture of a splendid white castle beside a loch.

'Very nice,' said Maggie McMuddle to Purpuss. 'But really! It's all very well her just taking a wee trip down here whenever she feels like it. But she never thinks of even asking me to go and have tea with her. I've never been to Drumtoochtie, and it would be nice, just once!'

Purpuss waved the tip of his tail as if to say:

'Yes. Quite so. Absolutely.'

But she liked having Cousin Annie Flora to stay, so she wrote back all the same and said, 'Yes, do come.' Then she dusted and polished the little yellow spare bedroom until even the floorboards under the bed shone. The curtains were freshly washed and ironed, and there was a big bunch of yellow daffodils in the glass vase on the bedside table.

'Perfect,' said Maggie McMuddle. 'Even Cousin Annie can't find anything to fuss about there. It's bright as a new pin.'

'Hmmm,' said Purpuss doubtfully. He was not all that fond of Cousin Annie Flora. She was such a fusspot, always tidying and plumping up cushions. He had been plumped up several times by accident on her last visit.

After breakfast Maggie McMuddle put on her good coat and tugged a comb through her hair, but it was no use, her fine fluffy white hair always looked as if

66

she had just been out for a walk in the
wind. She gave up and pulled on her big
green tartan beret.

'I have to meet the Drumtoochtie bus
now,' she said. 'Keep an eye on the house
while I'm away, Purpuss.'

'Hmmm,' said Purpuss, then he tippi-
toed upstairs for a peaceful snooze in the
middle of the big bed, just to hold the
quilt down. You never knew what quilts
might do without a sensible cat to keep
an eye on them.

The big blue bus was already there when Maggie McMuddle puffed up, and everyone was climbing out. Everyone except Cousin Annie Flora. She was thumping about inside, like a large bright pink blancmange. The driver seemed to be climbing over the seats, trying to help her.

'Yoohoo, dearie,' she called, leaning out of the window. 'Just getting all my wee parcels together. Just watch it with that heavy one, silly wee mannie, that's MY home-made fruitcake you're man-handling. And mind the squashy one. It's just a few wee scones, Maggie. And don't bounce the shoe box! Those are best brown farm eggs.'

At last she was off the bus, large and pink and puffing, with all her bags and parcels and the old brown suitcase tied with string.

'Oh my, it's that nice to see you again,' she said, hugging Maggie McMuddle and knocking her beret sideways. 'What do you fancy doing first? Something exciting I hope. I am chockered. Fed-up being stuck in the village all winter.'

Maggie McMuddle sighed. She had forgotten just how big and bouncy her cousin was. Suddenly, Annie Flora stopped talking and stood still.

'Here, look at that!' she said. 'A poster for a Mystery Coach Tour. Come on, let's go, Maggie. I feel like doing something really daft!'

'But your bags!' protested Maggie. 'We ought to take them home first.'

'No time. Coach leaves in twenty minutes. Come on, hurry up. My treat.'

Before she could catch her breath, Maggie McMuddle was bundled on to the Mystery Coach Tour and Cousin Annie was fussing and flapping, and pushing all her little parcels and packets up on to the luggage racks or beneath the seats.

'Oh, I can't wait,' she said. 'I haven't done anything really DARING for ages. Not since I dyed all my nighties shocking pink. You'll maybe have noticed I've decided to go pink this year. It's very fashionable, Maggie.

'Goodness!' said Maggie McMuddle,

quite at a loss to think what else to say.

'Well at least it should have been pink,' said Cousin Annie, 'except they came out a sort of streaky purple . . .' And she was off again, talking non-stop.

The bus began to fill up with other passengers. The driver came along to count them, and stopped and stared at Cousin Annie.

'Oh, I say,' said Maggie McMuddle. 'Isn't that the driver who. . .?'

But Cousin Annie didn't hear her. She was swapping cake recipes with the woman in the next seat.

The driver started up the engine. As they headed out of town, on to the open road, Maggie McMuddle rummaged in her bag for a peppermint, slipped her feet out of her shoes, crossed her hands in her lap and settled down to enjoy herself.

'It was a good idea this,' she said. 'It's lovely to see a little bit of countryside again.'

But Cousin Annie didn't hear her. She was busy telling the man behind her how to grow sunflowers.

The bus bounced along, twisting and turning, round country roads, through little villages, past farms and cottages, and a splendid white castle beside a loch.

'Isn't that the castle that was on your post card?' said Maggie McMuddle. But Cousin Annie didn't hear her. She was busy sorting out some knitting for a lady at the back of the bus.

'Nearly there now, folks!' called the driver, as he swung the coach round a bend in the road. Beneath them, snuggled among the hills, lay a little village with a church and a row of tiny cottages along the river bank.

'My, that is bonny!' said Maggie McMuddle. 'Look Annie. I think we're there.' Cousin Annie stopped talking at last, and glanced out of the window.

'What are we doing here?' she gasped.

'It's the end of the Mystery Coach Tour,' said Maggie McMuddle.

'But . . .but . . .' Cousin Annie was speechless.

The driver pulled up outside a red-roofed tea-room. Stood up and turned

round to address them.

'Right, ladies and gentlemen, here you are. Welcome to Drumtoochtie. You'll have plenty of time to look around, enjoy yourselves, and have a cup of tea.'

'Drumtoochtie?' squeaked Cousin Annie Flora. 'THAT'S the Mystery Coach Tour?'

Maggie McMuddle giggled. 'Well you did say you wanted to do something daft!' she said.

Cousin Annie Flora's face turned from purple to pink and then she sat down and laughed until she wobbled like a raspberry jelly.

'Come on,' she said at last, poking under the seat for the box of eggs. 'You bring the fruitcake and scones, they're up on the luggage rack. Now we're here we'll go back to my place, and I'LL make the afternoon tea today.'

And so she did.

'And what's more,' whispered Maggie McMuddle to Purpuss that night as she got ready for bed, back in her own house again. 'I liked it so much that she's

73

invited us to go up to Drumtoochtie for our holidays this year. What do you think of that then?'

'Hmmm!' said Purpuss, as he listened to Cousin Annie Flora snoring peacefully in the yellow bedroom. He had already been plumped up twice since she had arrived.

He settled down to sleep at the foot of Maggie McMuddle's bed, wondering if the corner café might give him a holiday job mouse hunting for two weeks.

7
Maggie McMuddle and the Great Canal Clean-up

If you walk down to the bottom of Antimacassar Street, past the allotments where Mr Brown grows his prize-winning tomatoes, and turn either right or left, you come on to the tow-path along the canal bank.

In the old days the canal used to be very busy with barges taking coal and iron to factories in the city. But now most of the factories have closed. Antimacassar Street is still busy, but the canal bank is very quiet. Wild flowers grow among the uncut grass, only swans and ducks crinkle the water. It could be very beautiful.

But it's not.

'The trouble is, Purpuss,' said Maggie McMuddle when she came back from her morning walk along the tow-path. 'The trouble is, folks just don't care. They drop their sweetie papers and crisp bags, and dump their piles of rubbish, and before you can say "tattie scone", the place just looks like a tip, and then nobody wants to tidy it up.'

She had told all the neighbours about it on the way home.

'Sorry,' said Mr Brown. 'Lots to do, lots to do, potting out just now.'

'Never really noticed it,' said Dozy Duncan. 'We always jog along the paths ourselves.'

'Haven't time to stop and look, two-three-four-five . . .' panted Mrs Duncan, jogging on the spot.

'I'd love to help,' said Sandy Sullivan, wiping his oily hands down his old over-alls. 'But I've got my bike to clean first.' Dolly and Pop were far too busy in the café.

'Is it REALLY as bad as that?' said Mrs Fairbairn. 'Someone should write to the local council. Of course I NEVER go down there myself, Fandango prefers the park. DON'T you, sweetie?' She bundled up the fat white poodle and clutched him to her furry jacket.

'So you see, Purpuss,' said Maggie

McMuddle. 'Nobody wants to know about it.'

'Hmrrr,' said Purpuss. For once he agreed with fat Fandango. He never went walking along the canal bank himself. Far too messy for a neat and natty cat.

'But I did find something for you amongst the rubbish,' said Maggie McMuddle, as she hung up her coat and handbag in the hall. 'Must have been lost by a child. I'm sure it's here in the bottom of my handbag. I'll just give it a wee wash first.'

'Hmmm?' said Purpuss, not too sure if he liked the idea of a rubbish present.

It was a little ball, made of clear plastic, with tiny orange gold flecks shining in it.

'I KNEW you would like it,' said Maggie McMuddle. 'It bounces like anything, and looks just like a little goldfish bowl if you hold it up to the light.'

'Hmmm,' said Purpuss. Really, she did have some funny ideas sometimes, he thought. He poked the ball with a paw, however, by way of being polite, and watched it roll across the floor.

Later that afternoon the milkman came round for the weekly money.

'Just a tick,' said Maggie McMuddle. 'I have it in my handbag.' But when she looked, there was no money there.

'Dearie me,' she said, hunting in the bottom of the bag. 'I know I had two five pound notes, I saw them when I opened my bag down by the canal bank this morning.'

She searched through all the little zipper pockets, twice.

'Oh, my!' she said. 'There's my other library ticket. I thought I'd lost that. I was just saying to Mrs Brown . . .'

'Let me see if I can find it,' said the milkman. He helped her search the bag a third time, right through every pocket, but there was still no sign of the five pound notes.

'Don't worry, Mrs Mac,' said the milkman as he went next door to the Browns. 'I'm sure it'll turn up, and you can always pay me next week.'

'Oh silly me!' she fussed, still rummaging in the bag. 'I MUST have dropped it down by the canal. I think I'll have to offer a reward to anyone who finds it.'

The milkman told Mr Brown what had happened.

'Down by the canal?' said Mr Brown. He watched the milkman cross the road to the Duncans, then he sat in front of the fire with his newspaper for a while thinking about it.

'I fancy a walk, Doris,' he said suddenly to Mrs Brown. 'Haven't been down the canal for ages. And let's take a rubbish bag with us, I hear it could do with tidying up.'

As they left the front garden they could see the milkman talking to Pop and Dolly outside the corner café. Sandy was sitting on the pavement, taking his motorbike to pieces, but he was listening.

Maggie McMuddle stood at her front window watching as the milkman went on to Mrs Fairbairn's house.

Dozy and Mrs Duncan gave her a wave as they pulled their front door shut behind them and set off down to the canal tow-path. They wore their matching blue gardening dungarees, and each carried a large empty plastic bag.

Maggie McMuddle smiled and nodded.

Purpuss sat up suddenly and snarled as Mrs Fairbarn flounced past, dragging Fandango on the lead behind her.

'It's lovely along the canal,' she was saying. 'Don't be such a picky poodle, you can go to the park any day. Coo-ee!'

She waved as she passed. Maggie McMuddle smiled and nodded.

Vurrrroooooooom! Sandy and his Dad gave a wave as they roared past on the motorbike, on their way down to the tow-path.

Maggie McMuddle smiled and nodded.

'Time to get some work done,' she said, and took out the vacuum to clean the hall carpet. Purpuss sat on the bottom step of the stairs, making sure she caught all the fluffballs and pointing out anything else she ought to pick up. When they finished that, she made a cup of tea and the two of them settled down to watch

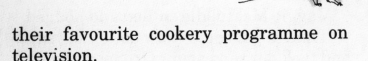

their favourite cookery programme on television.

Later, much later, Maggie McMuddle put on her coat again.

'I'm just going for a little walk along the canal bank to work up an appetite before tea,' she said to Purpuss. 'Would

you like to come with me this time?'
Purpuss stood up, yawned and stretched.

'Hmmm,' he said lazily, but he followed her out of the house and down the
road to the tow-path.

It was quiet in the street. No Mr
Brown in his front garden. No Duncans
jogging in their matching track suits. No

Sandy, sitting on the pavement by his motorbike.

It was very quiet in the street.

But when Maggie McMuddle turned the corner on to the tow-path – well, there was a surprise.

'Goodness, Purpuss,' she said. 'I can't remember when I've seen so many people down here. Look, there's Mrs Fairbairn with Fandango.'

'Tseeeeeee,' spat Purpuss hopping up on to a low stone wall. He sat and made faces at the fat poodle, which ignored him.

'Coo-ee!' Mrs Fairbairn. Have you lost something?'

'Eh? Beg pardon?' said Mrs Fairbairn.

'I thought maybe you had lost something, the way you were searching through the grass like that.' Maggie McMuddle smiled sweetly.

'No, no, just – clearing up some of the rubbish,' said Mrs Fairbairn, stuffing some empty crisp packets in a plastic bag. 'You're quite right, shocking state this path is in. Quite shocking.'

'But it looks so much tidier now,' said Maggie McMuddle.

A little further down the path she met Mr Brown. He had already filled two bags with rubbish, and must have gone back for his wheelbarrow, because he and Mrs Brown were struggling to load it with an old broken pram.

The Duncans, with the help of Pop Sullivan, had started a huge bonfire on an open patch of ground, and were piling on all sorts of scrap paper and wood.

'Oh goody! Can I help? I love bonfires,' said Maggie McMuddle, picking up some old chip papers. 'Isn't this fun? I'm so glad you all decided to come and help tidy up.'

'Er – well – yes . . .' said Dozy Duncan.

Sandy Sullivan came up just then, dragging along three large cardboard boxes.

'Here, Auntie Maggie,' he shouted. 'How much is the reward if we find your fivers?'

'Sandy!' hissed Pop Sullivan.

'Well that's why we came down, isn't it?' said Sandy. He smiled his big toothy grin. 'We've cleared all the way down the path, and nobody's found them yet. Can you remember exactly where you think you dropped them?'

'Well – yes . . .' said Maggie Mc-Muddle.

'Perhaps you could let Fandango have a sniff at your handbag, and then he could track them down,' said Mrs Fairbairn hopefully. Fandango lay in the middle of the path like a rumpled hearthrug.

'Oh no,' said Maggie McMuddle. 'I don't think so.' She looked at Purpuss, who almost seemed to be smiling.

'You see, they've already been found.'

'Where!' said everyone at once.

'We've searched the whole bank,' said Mr Brown.

'Thoroughly,' said the Duncans.

'At least twice,' said Pop Sullivan.

'Well I have anyway,' said Sandy, who had done most of the work.

'Oh, they weren't here at all,' laughed

Maggie McMuddle. 'I'm such a silly wee dumpling sometimes. I must have dropped them in the hall. Clever Purpuss found them, so as a special reward he's having a whole tin of sardines for tea tonight.'

She winked at Purpuss, and he might have winked back.

'Time the kettle was on,' she said.

'Well I never!' gasped Mr Brown.

They all stared at each other, and the bags of litter, and the bonfire and the rubbish piled high on Mr Brown's barrow.

Their laughter echoed along the quiet canal, as little plump Maggie McMuddle and fluffy ginger Purpuss set off to walk back to Antimacassar Street along the beautifully tidy canal tow-path.

Also by Moira Miller
available from Methuen

Oh Abigail!
Illustrated by Doreen Caldwell

Like all children, Abigail hates having to tidy her room or stop a favourite game just because it's bathtime. But then there are exciting visits to the zoo and the garden centre, also to a Christening and the great day of the Scouts' Jumble Sale. There is Abigail's alarm at her best toy, Hot Dog, going into the washing machine and her delight at being the proud owner of a brand new pair of bouncing boots.

Abigail is affectionate, imaginative, inquisitive and, of course, sometimes naughty – a thoroughly contemporary character with whom children and adults everywhere will love to identify.

Just Like Abigail!
Illustrated by Doreen Caldwell

Abigail is lovable, mischievous and always up to something! Whether she's sailing a boat in the park, looking at dinosaurs in a museum or waving a rattle on the football field, children will love her exploits.

It's Abigail Again
Illustrated by Doreen Caldwell

Abigail's back in action again! From taking part in a school concert to sleeping in a tent on her own, Abigail proves as irrepressible, and lovable, as ever!

What Size is Andy?
Illustrated by Doreen Caldwell

Andy is right in the middle of his family – too small to go out on his bike with Tivvy and Dave, but too big to go to the playgroup picnic with Todger and Rosie. However, he is just the right size for some things, as Tivvy and Dave discover when they take him out on Hallowe'en, and it's only Andy who manages to settle Gran into her new house.

These delightfully funny stories about a warm and loving family are ideal for reading aloud or for young readers to try for themselves.

Where Does Andy Go?
Illustrated by Doreen Caldwell

'We're going on holiday on a bus!' shouts
Andy to his friend Steve. 'We're going to
live on a bus.' 'Don't believe you!' shouts
back Steve. 'Nobody lives on a bus.'

But it's true! Andy, Dave, Tivvy, Rosie,
Todger, Mum, Dad and Uncle Billy are
off on holiday in a real double-decker bus
that leads them into lots of adventures –
and the best holiday ever!

Hamish and the Wee Witch
Illustrated by Mairi Hedderwick

An outstanding collection of stories in the folk tradition, each with a distinctive Scottish flavour. These gently humorous tales of Hamish and his encounters with the Wee Witch will delight and fascinate children of all ages.

Hamish and the Fairy Gifts
Illustrated by Mairi Hedderwick

Hamish and Mirren laughed when the old lady talked about the Wee Folk and all their mischief-making until their baby son disappeared . . .

Set on land and sea, peopled with mortals and fairies, ghosts and seals, these enchanting stories are the sequel to *Hamish and the Wee Witch*.